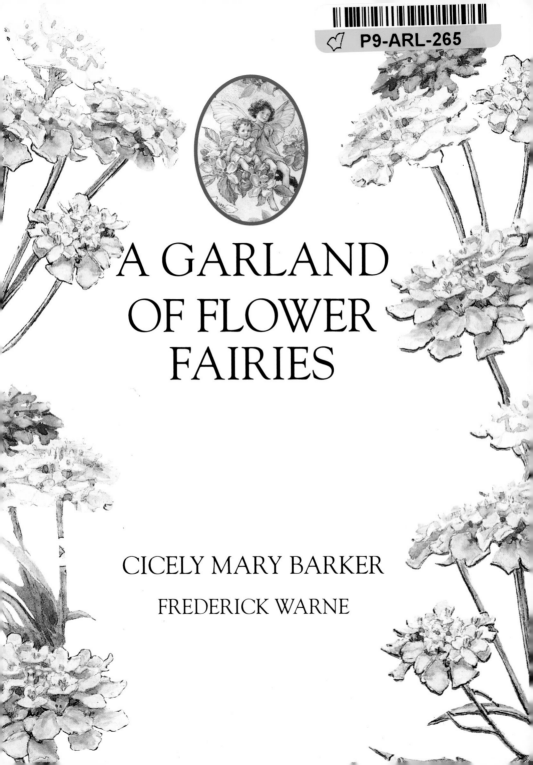

A GARLAND
OF FLOWER
FAIRIES

CICELY MARY BARKER

FREDERICK WARNE

*The reproductions in this book have been made using the most
modern electronic scanning methods from entirely new
transparencies of Cicely Mary Barker's original watercolours.
They enable Cicely Mary Barker's skill as an artist to be
appreciated as never before.*

FREDERICK WARNE
Published by the Penguin Group
Penguin Books Ltd, 27 Wrights Lane, London W8 5TZ, England
Penguin Books USA Inc., 375 Hudson Street, New York, N.Y. 10014, USA
Penguin Books Australia Ltd, Ringwood, Victoria, Australia
Penguin Books Canada Ltd, 10 Alcorn Avenue, Toronto, Ontario, Canada M4V 3B2
Penguin Books (N.Z.) Ltd, 182-190 Wairau Road, Auckland 10, New Zealand

Penguin Books Ltd, Registered Offices: Harmondsworth, Middlesex, England

First published 1994
3 5 7 9 10 8 6 4

ISBN 0 7232 4144 9

Colour reproduction by Saxon
Printed in China by Imago

◆MY PAGE◆

This Flower Fairies book belongs to

. . . .

My birthday is on . . . .

I am . . . . . . years and . . . . . . months old

My address is . . . .

. . . .

. . . .

My school is . . . .

My best friend's name is. . . . .

My favourite colour is. . . . .

My favourite Flower Fairy is . . . .

. . . .

◆ THE SONG OF ◆
THE CROCUS FAIRIES

Crocus of yellow, new and gay;
Mauve and purple, in brave array;
    Crocus white
    Like a cup of light,—
Hundreds of them are smiling up,
Each with a flame in its shining cup,
By the touch of the warm and welcome sun
Opened suddenly. Spring's begun!
Dance then, fairies, for joy, and sing
The song of the coming again of Spring.

The Crocus Fairies

The Tulip Fairy

◆ THE SONG OF ◆
THE TULIP FAIRY

Our stalks are very straight and tall,
    Our colours clear and bright;
Too many-hued to name them all—
    Red, yellow, pink, or white.

And some are splashed, and some, maybe,
    As dark as any plum.
From tulip-fields across the sea
    To England did we come.

We were a peaceful country's pride,
    And Holland is its name.
Now in your gardens we abide—
    And aren't you glad we came?

(But long, long ago, tulips were brought from Persian
gardens, before there were any in Holland.)

◆ THE SONG OF ◆
THE WILD CHERRY BLOSSOM

In April when the woodland ways
  Are all made glad and sweet
With primroses and violets
  New-opened at your feet,
    Look up and see
      A fairy tree,
    With blossoms white
      In clusters light,
All set on stalks so slender,
  With pinky leaves so tender.
O Cherry tree, wild Cherry tree!
  You lovely, lovely thing to see!

The Wild Cherry Blossom Fairy

Jasmine

The Jasmine Fairy

◆THE SONG OF ◆
THE JASMINE FAIRY

In heat of summer days
With sunshine all ablaze,
Here, here are cool green bowers,
Starry with Jasmine flowers;
Sweet-scented, like a dream
Of Fairyland they seem.

And when the long hot day
At length has worn away,
And twilight deepens, till
The darkness comes—then, still,
The glimmering Jasmine white
Gives fragrance to the night.

◆ THE SONG OF ◆
THE WILLOW FAIRY

By the peaceful stream or the shady pool
I dip my leaves in the water cool.

Over the water I lean all day,
Where the sticklebacks and the minnows play.

I dance, I dance, when the breezes blow,
And dip my toes in the stream below.

The Willow Fairy

The Snapdragon Fairy

◆ THE SONG OF ◆
THE SNAPDRAGON FAIRY

Into the Dragon's mouth he goes;
    Never afraid is he!
There's honey within for him, he knows,
    Clever old Bumble Bee!
The mouth snaps tight; he is lost to sight—
    How will he ever get out?
He's doing it backwards—nimbly too,
    Though he is somewhat stout!

Off to another mouth he goes;
    Never a rest has he;
He must fill his honey-bag full, he knows—
    Busy old Bumble Bee!
And Snapdragon's name is only a game—
    It isn't as fierce as it sounds;
The Snapdragon Elf is pleased as Punch
    When Bumble comes on his rounds!

◆ THE SONG OF ◆
THE POLYANTHUS AND
GRAPE HYACINTH FAIRIES

"How do you do, Grape Hyacinth?
    How do you do?"
"Pleased to see *you*, Polyanthus,
    Pleased to see *you*,
With your stalk so straight
    and your colours so gay."
"Thank you, neighbour!
    I've heard good news today."

"What is the news, Polyanthus?
    What have you heard?"
"News of the joy of Spring,
    In the song of a bird!"
"Yes, Polyanthus, yes,
    I heard it too;
That's why I'm here,
    with my bells in spires of blue."

The Polyanthus and Grape Hyacinth Fairies

The Ash Tree Fairy

◆ THE SONG OF ◆
THE ASH TREE FAIRY

Trunk and branches are smooth and grey;
 (Ash-grey, my honey!)
The buds of the Ash-tree, black are they;
 (And the days are long and sunny.)

The leaves make patterns against the sky,
 (Blue sky, my honey!)
And the keys in bunches hang on high;
 (To call them "keys" is funny!)

Each with its seed, the keys hang there,
 (Still there, my honey!)
When the leaves are gone
 and the woods are bare;
 (Short days may yet be sunny.)

◆ THE SONG OF ◆
THE ROSE HIP FAIRY

Cool dewy morning,
  Blue sky at noon,
White mist at evening,
  And large yellow moon;

Blackberries juicy
  For staining of lips;
And scarlet, O scarlet
  The Wild Rose Hips!

Gay as a gipsy
  All Autumn long,
Here on the hedge-top
  This is my song.

The Rose Hip Fairy

The Black Bryony Fairy

◆ THE SONG OF ◆
THE BLACK BRYONY FAIRY

Bright and wild and beautiful
For the Autumn festival,
I will hang from tree to tree
Wreaths and ropes of Bryony,
To the glory and the praise
Of the sweet September days.

(There is nothing black to be seen about this Bryony, but
people do say it has a black root; and this may be true,
but you would need to dig it up to find out. It used to be
thought a cure for freckles.)

◆ THE SONG OF ◆
THE SLOE FAIRY

When Blackthorn blossoms leap to sight,
They deck the hedge with starry light,
    In early Spring
    When rough winds blow,
    Each promising
    A purple sloe.

And now is Autumn here, and lo,
The Blackthorn bears the purple sloe!
    But ah, how much
    Too sharp these plums,
    Until the touch
    Of Winter comes!

(The sloe is a wild plum. One bite will set your teeth on
edge until it has been mellowed by frost; but it is not poisonous.)

The Sloe Fairy

The Pine Tree Fairy

◆ THE SONG OF ◆
THE PINE TREE FAIRY

A tall, tall tree is the Pine tree,
    With its trunk of bright red-brown—
The red of the merry squirrels
    Who go scampering up and down.

There are cones on the tall, tall Pine tree,
    With its needles sharp and green;
Small seeds in the cones are hidden,
    And they ripen there unseen.

The elves play games with the squirrels
    At the top of the tall, tall tree,
Throwing cones for the squirrels to nibble—
    I wish I were there to see!